Andrew Murray

JESUS HIMSELF

JESUS HIMSELF

BY

THE REV. ANDREW MURRAY.
Author of "Abide in Christ."

ISBN: 978-93-5128-385-0(HB)

First Published in 1893
Indian Reprint in 2017

Published by

Kalpaz Publications
C-30, Satyawati Nagar,
Delhi – 110052
E-mail: kalpaz@hotmail.com
Website: kalpazpublications.com
Ph.: +91-9212142040

Cataloging in Publication Data—DK

Courtesy: D.K. Agencies (P) Ltd. <docinfo@dkagencies.com>

Murray, Andrew, 1828-1917, **author.**

Jesus himself / by the Rev. Andrew Murray.

pages cm

"First published in 1893"

ISBN 9789351283850 (HB)

1. Jesus Christ—Significance. I. Title.

LCC BT295.M87 2017 | DDC 232 23

PREFACE.

The following brief messages comprise a revision of two addresses, which originally appeared in the *South African Pioneer*, the organ of the "Cape General Mission" (Rev. Andrew Murray, Pres.), and are published by arrangement, the Mission participating in the proceeds.

"Jesus Himself."

"*Their eyes were opened, and they knew Him.*"

I

THE words, from which I want to present a simple message, will be found in the Gospel according to St. Luke, the 24th chapter and the 31st verse: "*And their eyes were opened, and they knew Him.*" Some time since, I preached a sermon with the words "Jesus Himself" as the text; and as I went home I said to those who were walking with me: "How possible it is to have Jesus Himself with us and never to know it, and how possible to preach of, and to listen to, all the truth about

Jesus Himself and yet not to know Him." I cannot say what a deep impression was made upon me as I thought over it.

Now these disciples had spent a most blessed time with Jesus, but if they had gone away before He revealed Himself that evening, they would never have been sure that it was Jesus, for their eyes were holden that they should not know Him. That is, alas, the condition of a great multitude in the Church of Christ. They know that Christ has risen from the dead. They believe, and they very often have blessed experiences that come from the risen Christ. Very often in a time of Convention, or in time of silent Bible reading, or in a time of the visitation of God's grace, their hearts burn; and yet it can be said of a people whose hearts are burning within them, that they did not know it was Jesus Himself.

And now if you ask me what is to be the great blessing to be sought, my answer is this : Not only should we think about Jesus Himself and speak about Him and believe in Him, but we should come to the point that the disciples in the text arrived at, "and they knew Him." Everything is to be found in that.

If I read that story of the disciples on the way to Emmaus, I get from it four stages in the Christian life. Just think! How did they begin the morning that day? With

Hearts sad and troubled,

because they thought Jesus was dead. They did not know that He was alive, and that is the state of very many Christians. They look to the Cross, and they struggle to trust Christ, but they have never yet learned the blessedness of believing that there is a living Christ to do everything for them. Oh! that word of the angel to the women! "Why seek ye the living among the dead?" What is the difference between a dead Christ, whom the women went to anoint, and a living Christ? A dead Christ, I must do everything for; a living Christ does everything for me.

The disciples began the morning with a sad heart. I fancy very possibly they spent a sleepless night. Oh! the terrible disappointment! They had hoped that Christ would be the Deliverer of Israel, and they had seen Him die an accursed death. On the morning of that first day of the week, they rose with sad hearts — the bitter sadness cannot be expressed. That is just the life of many Christians. They try to believe in Jesus and to trust Him, and to hope in Him, but there is no joy. Why? Because they do not know that there is a living Christ to reveal Himself.

Then there is the second stage. What is that? The stage of which Christ speaks:

"Slow of heart to believe."

They had the message from the women. They told the stranger who walked with them: "Certain women have astonished us, telling us they have seen an angel, who says He is alive." And Christ replied to them: "Oh! fools, and slow of heart to believe." Yes! there are many Christians to-day who have heard and who know that they must not only believe in a crucified Christ, but in a living Christ, and they try to grasp it and take it in, but it does not bring them a blessing, and why? Because they want to feel it and not to believe it. They want to work for it, and with efforts get hold of it, instead of just quietly sinking down and believing, "Christ, the living Jesus, He will do *everything* for us." That is the second stage. The first stage is that of ignorance, the second stage is that of unbelief — the doubting heart that cannot take in the wonderful truth that Jesus lives.

Then comes the third stage —

The burning heart.

Jesus came to the two disciples, and after He had reproved them and said: "Oh! fools, and slow of heart to believe," He began to open the Scriptures to them, and to tell them of all the wonderful things the prophets had taught. Then their eyes were opened, and they began to understand the Scriptures. They saw that it was true that it was prophesied that Christ must rise. As He talked, there came out from Him — the living risen One — a mighty influence, and it rested upon them, and they began to feel their hearts burn within them with joy and gladness.

You still say perhaps: "That is the stage we want to come to." No ; God forbid you should stop there. You may get in that third stage — the burning heart — and yet something is still wanting — the revelation of Christ. The disciples had had a blessed experience of His divine powers, but He had not revealed Himself, and oh! how often it is that at Conventions and in churches, and in meetings and in blessed fellowship with God's saints, our hearts burn within us. These are precious experiences of the working of God's grace and Spirit, and yet there is something wanting. What is that? Jesus Himself has been working upon us, and the power of his risen life has touched us, but we cannot say, "I have met Him. He has made Himself known to me." Oh, the difference between a burning heart, which becomes cold after a time, which comes by fits and starts, and the blessed revelation of Jesus Himself as my Saviour, taking charge of me and blessing me and keeping me every day! This is the stage of

The satisfied heart.

Oh my brother, my sister! It is what I ask for you, and it is what I am sure you ask for yourself. I ask it for myself. Lord Jesus! may we know Thee in thy divine glory as the risen One, our Jesus, our Beloved and our mighty One. Oh! if there are any sad ones who cannot take this in, and who say, "I have never known the joy of religion yet"—listen, we are going to tell you how you can. All will center round this one thing, that just as a little child lives day by day in the arms of its mother, and grows up year by year under a mother's eye, it is a possibility that you can live every day and hour of your life in fellowship with the Holy Jesus.

He will do it for you.

Come, and let your sad heart begin to hope. Will He reveal Himself? He did it to the disciples and He will do it to you. Perhaps there are some who have got beyond the sad heart and who yet feel, "I have not got what I want." If you throw open your heart and give up everything but just believing and allowing Him to do what He wants, it will come. God be praised! it will come.

Jesus will reveal Himself.

Perhaps you have arrived at the stage of the burning heart, and can tell of many blessed experiences, but somehow there is a worm at the root. The experiences do not last, and the heart is so changeable. Oh come, my beloved! Follow Christ. Say, "Jesus, reveal Thyself that we may know Thee Thyself. We ask not only to drink of the living water, we want the fountain. We ask not only to bathe ourselves in the light, we want the Sun of Righteousness within our hearts. We ask not only to know Thee, who hast touched us and warmed our hearts and blessed us, but we want to know that we have the unchangeable Jesus dwelling within our hearts and abiding with us forevermore."

Now comes the question which I really wanted to put,—What are the conditions under which our blessed Lord reveals Himself? Or, put it this way,—To whom is it that Jesus will reveal Himself? We have only to see how he dealt with these disciples, and we get the answer. What is the answer? First of all I think I find here that Christ revealed Himself to those disciples

Who had given up everything for Him.

He had said to them: "Forsake all and follow Me," and they had done it. With all their feebleness and all their unfaithfulness they followed Christ to the end. He said to them: "Ye have continued with Me in My temptations, and I appoint you a kingdom, as I have received a kingdom from My Father." They were not perfect men, but they would have died for Him. They loved Him, they obeyed Him, they followed Him. They had left all, and for three years they had been following hard after Christ. You say "Tell me what Christ wants of me, if I am to have his wonderful presence. Tell me what is the character of the man to whom Christ will reveal Himself in this highest and fullest way?" I answer: "It is the one who is ready to forsake all and to follow Him." If Christ is to give Himself wholly to me, He must know that He has me wholly for Himself; and I trust God will give grace that these words spoken about the consecration and the surrender, not only of all evil, but of many lawful things, and even, if necessary, of life itself, may lead us to understand what the demand is that Jesus makes upon us.

The motto of the Cape General Mission is,

"God first."

In one sense that is a beautiful motto, and yet I am not always satisfied with it, because it is a motto that is often misunderstood. God first may mean "I" second, something else third, and something else fourth. God is thus first in order, but still God becomes one of a series of powers, and that is not the place God wants. The meaning of the words, "God first" is really "God all; God everything;" and that is what Christ wants. To be willing to give up everything, to submit to Christ to teach him what to say and what to do, is the first mark of the man to whom Christ will come. Are you not ready to take this step and say: "Jesus! I do give up everything; I have given up everything; reveal Thyself."

Oh, brother! oh, sister! do not hesitate. Speak it out in your heart, and let this be the time in which a new sacrifice shall be laid at the feet of the blessed Lamb of God.

There is a second thought. There is first the idea of having forsaken all to follow Him; of having given up everything in obedience to Him, and living just a life of simple love and obedience. But there is a second thing needed in the man who is to have this full revelation of Christ. He must be

Convicted of his unbelief.

"Oh! fools, and slow of heart to believe what the prophets have said." Oh! brother, sister, if we could have a sight of the amount of unbelief in the hearts of God's children, barring the door and closing the heart against Christ, how we should stand astonished and ashamed! When there is not unbelief but where there is faith, Christ cannot help coming in. He cannot help coming where there is a living faith, a full faith. The heart is opened, the heart is prepared; and as naturally as water runs into a hollow place, so naturally Christ must come into a heart that is full of faith. What is the hindrance with some earnest souls, who say: "I have given myself up to the Lord Jesus. I havo done it often, and by His grace I am doing it every day, and God knows how earnestly and really I am doing it, and I have the sanction of God upon it, I know God has blessed me"? They have not been convicted of their unbelief. "Oh! fools, and slow of heart to believe." Do you know what Christ said about a man calling his brother a fool? Yet here the loving Son of God could find no other word to speak to His beloved disciples: "Oh! fools, and slow of heart to believe." You want the Lord Jesus to give you this full revelation of Himself? Are you willing to acknowledge that you are a fool for never having believed in Him? "Lord Jesus, it is my own fault. There Thou art, longing to have possession of me. There Thou hast been with Thy faithful promises waiting to reveal Thyself."

Did you ever hear of a man loving another and not longing to reveal himself? Christ longs to reveal Himself, but He cannot on account of our unbelief. May God convict us of our unbelief that we may get utterly ashamed and broken down, and cry, "Oh, my God, what is this, this heart of unbelief actually throwing a barrier across the door that Christ cannot step in, blinding my eyes that I cannot see Jesus, though he is so near? Here He has been for ten or twenty years, from time to time giving me the burning heart, enjoying the experience of a little of His love and grace, and yet I have not had the revelation of Him, taking possession of my heart and dwelling with me in unbroken continuity." Oh! may God convict us of unbelief. Do let us believe because all things are possible to him that believes. That is God's word, and this blessing, receiving the revelation of Jesus, can come only to those who learn to believe and to trust him.

There is another mark of those to whom this special revelation of Christ will come, and that is,

They do not rest until they obtain it.

You know the story. Their hearts were burning as they drew nigh to the place they were going to, and Christ made as if He were going farther. He put them to the test, and if they had allowed Him quietly to go on, if they had been content with the experience of the burning heart, they would have lost something infinitely better. But they were not content with it. They were not content to go home to the disciples that night and say, "Oh, what a blessed afternoon we have had! What wonderful teaching we have had!" No! The burning heart and the blessed experience just made them say, "Lord, abide with us," and they compelled Him to come in. They constrained Him to come in.

It always reminds me of the story of Jacob, "I will not let Thee go, except Thou bless me." That is the spirit that prepares us for the revelation of Jesus. Oh! my dear friend, has this been the spirit in which we have looked upon the wonderful blessing that we have sometimes heard of? "Oh! my Lord Jesus, though I do not understand it, though I cannot grasp it, though my struggles avail nothing, I am not going to let Thee go. If it is possible for a sinner on earth to have Jesus every day, every hour, and every moment in resurrection power dwelling in his heart, shining within him, filling him with love and joy,—if that is possible, I want it."

Is that your language?

Oh! come then and say: "Lord Jesus, I cannot let Thee go except Thou bless me." The question is asked so often: "What is the cause of the feeble life of so many Christians?" What is really the matter? What is actually the want?

How little the Church responds to Christ's call! how little the Church is what Christ would have her to be! What is the cause of all the trouble? Various answers may be given, but there is one answer which includes all the other answers, and that is, each believer wants the personal

Full revelation of a personal Christ as an indwelling Lord, as a satisfying portion. When the Lord Jesus was here upon earth, what was it that distinguished His disciples from other people? He took them away from their fish-nets, and from their homes, and He gathered them about Himself, and they knew Jesus. He was their Master, and guarded them, and they followed Him. And what is to make a difference between Christ's disciples — not those who are just hoping to get to heaven, but Christ's whole-hearted disciples — what is to make a difference between them and other people? It is this, to be in fellowship with Jesus — every hour of the day; and just as Christ upon earth was able to keep those people with Him for three years, day by day, so

Christ is able

in heaven now to do what He could not do when He was on earth — to keep in the closest fellowship with every believer throughout the whole world. Glory be to God! You know that text in Ephesians: "He that descended is the same also that ascended, that He might fill all things." Why was my Lord Jesus taken up to heaven away from the life of earth? Because the life of earth is a life confined to localities, but the life in heaven is a life in which there is no limit and no bound and no locality, and Christ was taken up to heaven, that, in the power of God, of the omnipresent God, He might be able to fill every individual here and be with every individual believer.

That is what my heart wants to realize by faith ; that is a possibility, that is a promise, that is my birthright, and I want to have it, and I want by the grace of God to say, "Jesus, I will not rest until Thou hast revealed Thyself fully to my soul."

There are often very blessed experiences in the Christian life in what I call the third stage — the stage of the burning heart. Do you know what another great mark of that stage is? Delight in God's word. How did the disciples get their burning hearts? By that strange opening of the Scripture to them. He made it all look different, — new, — and they saw what they had never seen before. They could not help feeling,

How wonderful,

how heavenly was that teaching. Oh! there are many Christians who find the best time of the day is the time when they can get with their Bibles, and who love nothing so much as to get a new thought; and as a diamond digger rejoices when he has found a diamond, or a gold digger when he has found a nugget, they delight when they get from the Bible some new thought, and they feed upon it. Yet with all that interest in God's word, and with all that stirring of the heart with joy, when they go into business or attend to their daily duties, there is still something wanting.

We must come away from all the manifold and multifarious blessings that Jesus can bestow from time to time, to the blessed unity of that one—

that Jesus makes Himself known, Jesus Himself is willing to make Himself known. Oh! if I were to ask, "Is not this just what you and I want, and what many of us have been longing for?" I am sure you would answer,

"That is what I want."

Think what the blessedness will be that comes from it. You often sing:—

"Oh! the peace my Saviour gives!
Peace I never knew before,
And my way has brighter grown,
Since I've learnt to trust Him more."

I recently had a letter from some one in the Free State saying what a wonderful comfort and strength that little verse was in the midst of difficulties and troubles. Yes; but how can that peace be kept? It was the presence of Christ that brought the peace. When the storm was threatening to swallow up the disciples, it was the presence of Christ Himself that gave the peace.

Oh! Christian, do you want peace and rest? You must have Jesus Himself. You talk of purity, you talk of cleansing, you talk of deliverance from sin. Praise God, here is the deliverance and the cleansing, when the living Jesus comes and gives power. Then we have this resurrection of Christ, this heavenly Christ upon the throne, making Himself known to us. Surely that will be the secret of purity and the secret of strength.

Where does the strength of so many come from? From the joy of a personal friendship with Jesus. Those disciples, if they had gone away with their burning hearts to the other disciples, could have told them wonderful things of a man who had explained to them the Scriptures and the promises, but they could not have said, "We have seen Jesus." They might have said, "Jesus is alive. We are sure of that," but that would not have satisfied the others. But they could now go and say,

"We have seen Himself.

He has revealed Himself to us." We are all glad to work for Christ, but there is a complaint throughout the Church of Christ, from the ministers in the pulpit down to the feeblest worker, of lack of joy and lack of blessedness. Let us try and find out whether this is not the place where the secret will be discovered — that the Lord Jesus comes and shows Himself to us as our Master and speaks to us. When we have Jesus with us, and when we go every footstep with the thought that it is Jesus wants us to go, it is Jesus who sends us and is helping us, then there will be brightness in our testimony, and it will help other believers, and they will begin to understand; "I see why I have failed. I took the word, I took the blessing, and I took, as I thought, the life, but I was without the living Jesus."

And if you now ask, "How will this revelation come?" Brother, sister, that is the secret that no man may tell, that Jesus keeps to Himself. It is

In the power of the Holy Ghost; Christ, the risen One, entered into a new life. His resurrection life is entirely different from His life before His death. You know what we read: "They knew Him." He revealed Himself, and then He passed away. And was that vision of Christ worth so much? It was lost in a moment. It was worth heaven, eternity, everything. Why? Because henceforth Christ was no longer to be known after the flesh. Christ was henceforth in the power of the Spirit, which fills Heaven; in the power of the Spirit which is the power of the Godhead; in the power of the Spirit, which fills our hearts. Christ was henceforth to live in the life of Heaven.

Thank God, Christ can by the power of the Holy Ghost reveal Himself to each one of us; but oh! brother, it is a secret thing between Christ and yourself. Take this assurance, "Their eyes were opened and they knew Him," and believe that it is written for you.

You say, "I have known the other three stages; the stage of the sad heart, mourning that I knew no living

Christ; I have known the stage of the slow heart to believe, when I struggled with my unbelief; and I know the stage of the burning heart, when there are great times of joy and blessedness." You say that? Oh come then and know the fourth stage of

The satisfied heart,

of the heart made glad for eternity, of the heart that cannot keep its joy in, but goes away back to Jerusalem, and says, "It is true. Jesus has revealed Himself. I know it, I feel it." Oh! brother, oh! sister, how will this revelation come? Jesus will tell you. Just come to the Lord Jesus and breathe up before Him a simple child-like prayer, and I, His servant, will come and take you by the hand and say: "Come, now, my work is done. I have pointed to the Lamb of God, to the risen One. My work is done."

Let us enter into the Holy Presence and begin, if you have never yet sought it before, begin to plead: "Oh! Saviour, that I might have this blessedness every moment present with me—Jesus Himself, my portion forever."

"Jesus Himself."

"Lo, I am with you alway."

II

WHEN I think of all the struggles and difficulties and failures of which many complain, and know that many are trying to make a new effort to begin a holy life, their hearts fearing all the time that they would fail again, owing to so many difficulties and temptations and the natural weakness of their character, my heart longs to be able to tell them in words so simple that a little child could understand,

What the secret is of the Christian life.

And then the thought comes to me, Can I venture to hope that it will be given to me to take that glorious, heavenly, divine Lord Jesus and to show Him to these souls, so that they can see Him in His glory? And can it be given to me to open their eyes to see that there is a Divine, Almighty Christ, who does actually come into the heart and who faithfully promises, "I will come and dwell with you, and I will never leave you?" No; my words cannot do that. But then I thought, my Lord Jesus can use me as a simple servant to take such feeble ones by the hand and encourage and help them; to say, Oh, come, come, come, into the presence of Jesus and wait on Him, and He will reveal Himself to thee. I pray God that He may use His precious Word. It is simply

The presence of the Lord Jesus. That is the secret of the Christian's strength and joy. You know that when He was upon earth, He was present in bodily form with his disciples. They walked about together all day, and at night they went into the same house, and sometimes slept together and ate and drank together. They were continually together. It was the presence of Jesus that was the training school of His disciples. They were bound to Him by that wonderful intercourse of love during three long years, and in that intercourse they learned to know Christ, and Christ instructed and corrected them, and prepared them for what they were afterward to receive. And now when He is going away, He says to them: "Lo, behold, I am with you always—all the days—even unto the end of the world."

What a promise! And just as really as Christ was with Peter in the boat, just as Christ sat with John at the table, as really can I have Christ with me. And more really, for they had their Christ in the body and He was to them a man, an individual separate from them, but I may have glorified Christ in the power of the throne of God, the omnipotent Christ, the omnipresent Christ.

What a promise! You ask me, How can that be? And my answer is, Because Christ is God, and because Christ after having been made man, went up into the throne and the Life of God. And now that blessed Christ Jesus, with His loving, pierced heart;

that blessed Jesus Christ, who lived upon earth; that same Christ glorified into the glory of God, can be in me and

Can be with me all the days.

You say, Is it really possible for a man in business, for a woman in the midst of a large and difficult household, for a poor man full of care; is it possible? Can I always be thinking of Jesus? Thank God, you need not always be thinking of Him. You may be the manager of a bank, and your whole attention may be required to carry out the business that you have to do. But thank God, while I have to think of my business, Jesus will think of me, and He will come in and will take charge of me. That little child, three months old, as it sleeps in its mother's arms, lies helplessly there; it hardly knows its mother, it does not think of her, but the mother thinks of the child. And this is the blessed mystery of love, that Jesus the God-man waits to come in to me in the greatness of His love; and as He gets possession of my heart, He embraces me in those divine arms and tells me, "My child, I the Faithful One, I the Mighty One will abide with thee, will watch over thee and keep thee all the days." He tells me He will come into my heart, so that I can be a happy Christian, a holy Christian, and a useful Christian. You say, Oh! if I could only believe that, if I could think that it is possible to have Christ always, every hour, every moment with me,

Taking and keeping charge of me!

My brother, my sister, it is just literally this that is my message to you. When Jesus said to His disciples,

"Lo, I am with you always," He meant it in the fullness of the divine Omnipresence, in the fullness of the divine love, and he longs to-night to reveal Himself to you and to me as we have never seen Him before.

And now just think a moment what a blessed life that must be—the presence of Jesus always abiding. Is not that the secret of peace and happiness? If I could just attain (that is what each heart says) to that blessed state in which every day and all the day I felt Jesus to be watching and ever keeping me, oh, what peace I would have in the thought, "I have no care if He cares for me, and I have no fear if He provides for me." Your heart says that this is too good to be true, and that it is too glorious to be for you. Still you acknowledge it must be most blessed,

Fearful one, erring one, anxious one, I bring you God's promise, it is for me and for you. Jesus will do it; as God, He is able, and Jesus is willing and longing as the Crucified One to keep you in perfect peace. This is a wonderful fact, and it is the secret of joy unspeakable.

And this is also

The secret of Holiness.

Instead of indwelling sin, an indwelling Christ conquering it; instead of indwelling sin, the indwelling life and light and love of the blessed Son of God. He is the secret of holiness. "Christ is made unto us sanctification." Remember that it is Christ Himself who is made unto us sanctification. Christ coming into me, taking charge of my whole being; my nature and my thoughts and my affections and my will ; ruling all things. It is this that will make me holy. We talk about holiness, but do you know what holiness is? You have as much holiness as you have of Christ, for it is written, "Both he that sanctifieth and they who are sanctified are all of one;" and Christ sanctifies by bringing God's life into me.

We read in Judges, "The Spirit of the Lord clothed Gideon." But you know that there is in the New Testament an equally wonderful text, where we read, "Put on the Lord Jesus Christ," that is, clothe yourself with Christ Jesus. And what does that mean? It does not only mean, by imputation of righteousness outside of me, but to clothe myself with the living character of the living Christ, with the living love of the living Christ.

Put on the Lord Jesus.

Oh! what a work. I cannot do it unless I believe and understand that He whom I have to put on is as a garment covering my whole being. I have to put on a living Christ who has said, "Lo, I am with you all the days." Just draw the folds closer round you, of that robe of light with which Christ would array you. Just come and acknowledge that Christ is with you, on you, in you. Oh, put Him on! And when you look at one characteristic of His after another; and you hear God's word, "Let this mind be in you which was also in Jesus Christ," and it tells you He was obedient unto the death; and then you answer, Christ the obedient one, Christ whose whole life was obedience, it is that Christ whom I have received and put on. He becomes my life and His obedience rests upon me, until I learn to whisper as Jesus did, "My Father, Thy will be done; lo, I come to do Thy will."

This, too, is the secret of influence in witness and work. How comes it that it is so

Difficult to be obedient,

and how comes it that I so often sin? People sing, "Oh, to be wholly Thine," and sing it from their hearts. How comes it then that they are disobedient again? Where does the disobedience come from? And the answer comes, It is because I am trying to obey a distant Christ, and thus His commands do not come with power. Look what I find in God's Word. When God wanted to send any man upon His service, He first met him and talked with him and cheerd him time after time. God appeared to Abraham seven or eight times, and gave to him one command after another; and so Abraham learned to obey Him perfectly. God appeared to Joshua and to Gideon, and they obeyed. And why are we not obedient? Because we have so little of this near intercourse with Jesus. But, oh, if we knew

This blessed, Heavenly secret

of having the presence of Christ with us every day, every hour, every minute, what a joy it would be to obey! We could not walk in this consciousness,—My Lord Jesus is with me and around me,—and not obey Him! Oh, do you not begin to long and say, This is what I must have, the ever-abiding presence of Jesus! There are some Christians who try not to be disobedient, who come to their Sunday and week-day duties most faithfully, and pray for grace and a blessing, and they complain of so little blessing and power, so little power! And why? Because there is not enough of the living Jesus in their hearts. I sometimes think of this as a most solemn truth. There is a great diversity of gifts amongst ministers and others who speak; but I am sure of this, that a man's gifts are not the measure of his real power. I am sure of this, that God can see what neither you nor I can see. Sometimes people feel something of it; but in proportion as a man has in reality, not as a sentiment or an aspiration, or a thought, but in reality, the very spirit and presence of Jesus upon him, there comes out from him an unseen silent influence. That secret influence is the

Holy presence of Jesus.

"Lo, I am with you always." And now, if what I have said has sufficed just to indicate what a desirable thing it is, what a blessed thing it is to live for, then let me now give you an answer to the question that arises in more than one heart. I can hear some one say, "Tell me how I can get this blessed abiding presence of Jesus; and when I have got it, how I can ever keep it. I think if I have this, I have all. The Lord Jesus has come very near to me. I have tried to turn away from everything that can hinder, and have had my Lord very near. But how can I know that He will be with me always?" If you were to ask the

Lord, "Oh, my blessed Lord Christ, what must I do, how can I enjoy Thy never-failing presence?" His first answer would be, "Only believe. I have said it often, and you only partly understood it, but I will say it again—

My child, only believe."

It is by faith. We sometimes speak of faith as trust, and it is a very helpful thing to tell men that faith is trust: but when people say, as they sometimes do, that it is nothing else but trust, that is not the case. It is a far wider word than trust. It is by faith that I learn to know the invisible One, the invisible God, and that I see Him. Faith is my spiritual eye-sight for the unseen and heavenly. You often try hard to trust God, and you fail. Why? Because you have not taken time first to see God. How can you trust God fully until you have met Him and known Him? You ask, "Where ought I to begin?" You ought to begin with first believing; with presenting yourself before this God in the attitude of silent worship, and asking Him to let a sense of His greatness and His presence come upon you. You must ask Him to let your heart be covered over with his holy presence. You must seek to realize in your heart the presence of an Almighty and all-loving God, an unspeakably loving God. Take time to worship Him as the omnipotent God, to feel that the very power that created the world, the very power that raised Jesus from the dead, is at this moment working in your heart. We do not experience it because we do not believe. We must take time to believe. Jesus says, "Oh, my child, shut your eyes to the world, and shut out of your heart all these thoughts about religion, and begin to believe in God Himself." That is the first article of the Creed — "I believe in God."

By believing I open my heart.

to receive this glorious God, and I bow and worship. And then as I believe this, I look up and I see the Lamb upon the Throne, and I believe that the Almighty power of God is in Jesus for the very purpose of revealing His presence to my heart. Why are there two upon the Throne? Is not God enough? The Lamb of God is upon the Throne in your interest and in mine; the Lamb upon the Throne is Christ Himself, with power as God to take possession of me. Oh, do not think you cannot get that realization. And do not think of it as now only within your reach; but cultivate the habit of faith. "Jesus, I believe in Thy glory; I believe in Thine omnipotence; I believe in Thy power working within me. I believe in Thy living, loving presence with me, revealing itself in Divine power."

Do not be occupied with feelings or experiences. You will find it far simpler and easier just to trust and say, "I am sure He is all for me." Get rid of yourself for the time; do n't think or speak about yourself; but

Think what Jesus is.

And then remember it is believe always. I sometimes feel that I cannot find words to tell how God wants His people to believe from morning till night. Every breath ought to be just believing.

Yes, it is indeed true; the Lord Jesus loves us to be just believing from morning to evening, and you must begin to make that the chief thing in life. In the morning when you wake, let your heart go forth with a large faith in this; and in the watches of the night let this thought be present with you — my Saviour Jesus is round me and near me, and you can look up and say, "I want to trust Thee always." You know what trust is. It is so sweet to trust. And now cannot you trust Jesus; this presence, this keeping presence? He lives for you in Heaven. You are marked with His blood, and he loves you; and cannot you say, "My King, my King, He is with me all the days?" Oh, trust Jesus to fulfill His own promises.

There is a second answer that I think

Christ would give if we come to Him believing, and say, "Is there anything more, my blessed Master?" I think I can hear His answer:

"My child, always obey."

Do not fail to understand the lesson contained in this one word. You must distinctly and definitely take that word OBEY and obedience, and learn to say for yourselves: "Now I have to obey, and by the grace of God I am going to obey in everything." At our recent exhibition at the Cape, Mr. Rhodes, our Prime Minister, went to the gate, thinking he had got the fee in his pocket. When he got to the gate, however, he found he had not enough money, and said to the door-keeper, "I am Mr. Rhodes; let me in and I will take care you do not suffer." But the man said, "I cannot help that, sir, I have my orders," and he refused to let Mr. Rhodes in. He had to borrow from a friend, and pay before he could pass the gate. At a dinner afterward Mr. Rhodes spoke about it, and said it was a real joy to see a man stick to his order like that. That is it. The man had his orders, and that was enough to him, and whoever came to the gate had to pay his fee before he could enter. God's children ought to be like soldiers, and be

Ready to say, "I must obey."

Oh! to have that thought in our hearts—"Jesus, I love to obey Thee." There must be personal intercourse with the Saviour, and then comes the joy of personal service and allegiance. Are you ready to obey in all feebleness and weakness and fear? Can you say,

"Yes, Lord Jesus, I will obey?" If so, then give yourself up absolutely. Then your feeling will be, "I am not going to speak one word if I think that Jesus would not like to hear it." I am not going to have an opinion of my own, but my whole life is to be covered with the purity of His obedience to the Father and His self-sacrificing love to me. I want Christ to have my whole life, my whole heart, my whole character. I want to be like Christ and to obey." Give yourself up to this loving obedience.

The third thought is this: If I say, "My Master, blessed Saviour, tell me all, I will believe, I do obey, and I will obey. Is there anything more I need to secure the enjoyment of Thine abiding presence?" And I catch this answer:

"My child, close intercourse with me every day."

Ah, there is the fault of many who try to obey and try to believe; they do it in their own strength, and they do not know that if the Lord Jesus is to reign in their hearts, they must have close communion with Him every day. You cannot do all He desires, but Jesus will do it for you. There are many Christians who fail here, and on that account do not understand what it is to have fellowship with Jesus. Do let me try and impress this upon you: God has given you a loving, living Saviour, and how can He bless if you do not meet Him? The joy of friendship is found in intercourse; and Jesus asks for this every day, that he may have time to influence me, to tell me of Himself, to teach me, to breathe His Spirit unto me, to give me new life and joy and strength. And remember, intercourse with Jesus

Does not mean half-an-hour

or an hour in your closet. A man may study his Bible or his commentary carefully; he may look up all the parallel passages in the chapter; when he comes out of his closet he may be able to tell you all about it, and yet he has never met Jesus that morning at all. You have prayed for five or ten minutes, and you have never met Jesus. And so we must remember that though the Bible is most precious, and the reading of it most blessed and needful; yet prayer and Bible reading are not fellowship with Jesus. What we need every morning is to meet Jesus, and to say, "Lord, here is the day again, and I am just as weak in myself as ever I was;

do Thou come and feed me this morning with Thyself and speak to my soul." Oh, friends, it is not your faith that will keep you standing, but it is a living Jesus, met

Every day in fellowship

and worship and love. Wait in His presence, however cold and faithless you feel. Wait before Him and say: "Lord, helpless as I am, I believe and rest in the blessed assurance that what Thou hast promised Thou wilt do for me."

I ask my Master once again, "Lord Jesus, is that all?" And his answer is: "No, my child; I have one thing more." "And what is that? Thou hast told me to believe, and to obey, and to abide near to Thee: what wouldst Thou have more?"

"Work for me, my child. Remember, I have redeemed thee for My service; I have redeemed thee to have a witness to go out into the world confessing Me before men." Oh, do not hide your treasure, or think that if Jesus is with you, you can hide it. One of two things will happen — either you must give all up, or it must come out. You have perhaps heard of the little girl, who, after one of Mr. Moody's meetings, was found to be singing some of the hymns we all know. The child's parents were in a good position in society, and while singing those hymns in the drawing-room her mother forbade her. One day she was singing the hymn "Oh, I'm so glad that Jesus loves me," when her mother said, "My child, how is it that you sing this when I have forbidden it?" She replied, "Oh, mother, I cannot help it; it comes out of itself." If Jesus Christ be in the heart, He must come out. Remember, it is not only our duty to confess Him; it is that, but it is something more. If you do not do it, it is just an indication .that you have not given yourself up to Jesus; your character, your reputation, your all. You are holding back from Him. You must confess Jesus in the world, in your home; and in fact everywhere. You know the Lord's command, "Go ye into all the world, and preach the Gospel to every creature;" "and, lo, I am with you," meaning, "Any one may work for Me, and I will be with him." It is true of the minister, the missionary, and every believer who works for Jesus. The presence of Jesus is intimately connected with work for Him. You say, "I have never thought of that before. I have my Sunday work, but during the week I am not doing work for Him." You cannot have the presence of Jesus, and let this continue to be the case. I do not believe you could have the presence of Jesus all the week and yet do nothing for Him; therefore my advice is, work for Him who is worthy, His blessing and His presence will be found in the work. It is

A blessed privilege to work for Christ

in this perishing world. Oh, why is it that our hearts often feel so cold and closed up, and so many of us say, "I do not feel called to Christ's work"? Be willing to yield yourself for the Lord's service, and He will reveal Himself to you.

Christ comes with His wondrous promise, and what He says, He says to all believers: "Lo, I am with you always; that is My promise; this is what I in My power can do; this is what I faithfully engage to perform; will you have it?

I give Myself to thee, O soul."

To each of those who have come to Him, Christ says, "I give Myself to thee, to be absolutely and wholly thine every hour of every day; to be with thee and in thee every moment, to bless thee and sustain thee, and to give thee each moment the consciousness of My presence; I will be wholly, wholly, wholly thine."

And now, what is the other side? He wants me to be wholly His. Are you ready to take this as your motto now,

"Wholly for God"?

O God, breathe Thou Thy presence in my heart that Thou mayest shine forth from my life. "Wholly for God," let this be our motto. Come let us cast ourselves on our faces before His feet. Our missionary from Nyassaland says he has often been touched by seeing how the native Christians, when they are brought to Jesus, do not stand in prayer; they do not kneel; but they cast themselves upon the earth with their foreheads to the ground, and there they lie, and with loud voices cry unto God. I sometimes feel that I wish we could do that ourselves; but we need not do it literally. Let us do it in spirit, for the everlasting Son of God has come into our hearts. Are you going to take Him and to keep Him there, to give Him glory and let Him have His way? Come now and say, "I will seek Thee with my whole heart; I am wholly Thine." Yield yourself entirely to Him to have complete possession. He will take and keep possession. Come now. Jesus delights in the worship of His Saints. Our whole life can become one continuous act of worship and work of love and joy, if we only remember and value this, that Jesus has said, "Lo, I am with you all the days, even unto the end of the world."